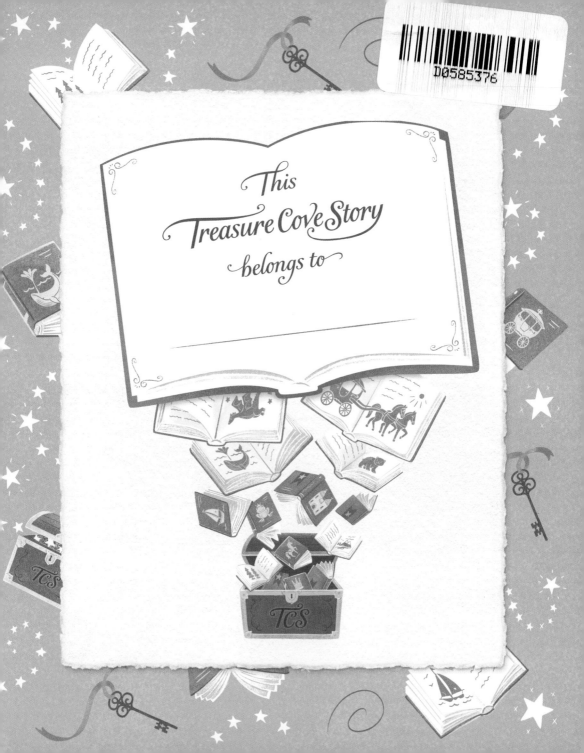

This
Treasure Cove Story
belongs to

_____

TOY STORY
THE PET PROBLEM

A CENTUM BOOK 978-1-912396-65-8
Published in Great Britain by Centum Books Ltd.
This edition published 2018.

3 5 7 9 10 8 6 4 2

Centum Books Ltd, 20 Devon Square, Newton Abbot,
Devon, TQ12 2HR, UK.

www.centumbooksltd.co.uk | books@centumbooksltd.co.uk
CENTUM BOOKS Limited Reg.No. 07641486.

A CIP catalogue record for this book is available
from the British Library.

Printed in China.

A Treasure Cove Story

Disney · PIXAR

TOY STORY

The Pet Problem

Written by Kristen L Depken
Illustrated by Caroline LaVelle Egan

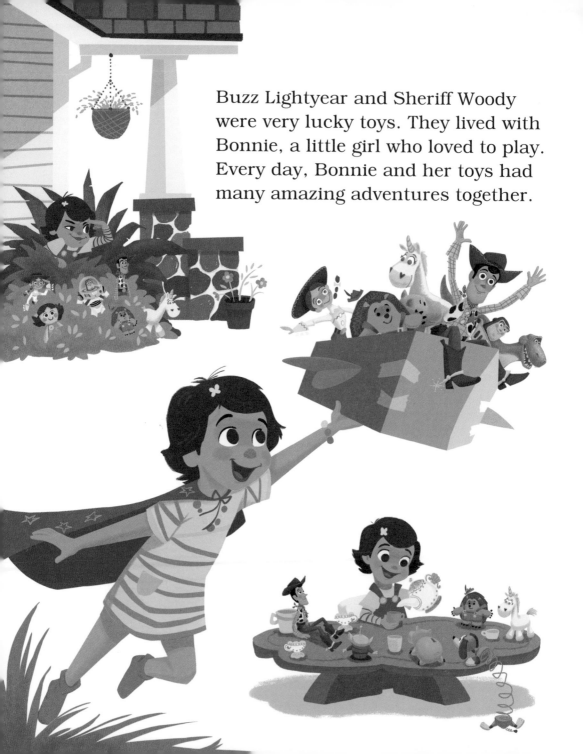

Buzz Lightyear and Sheriff Woody were very lucky toys. They lived with Bonnie, a little girl who loved to play. Every day, Bonnie and her toys had many amazing adventures together.

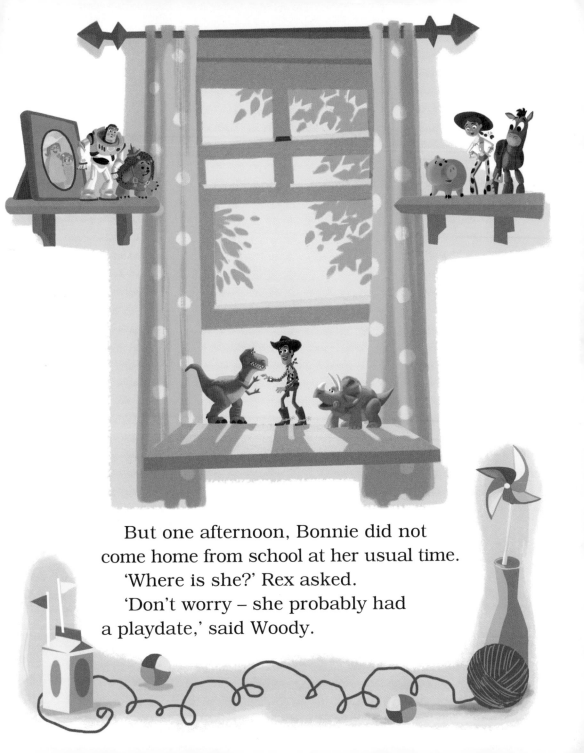

But one afternoon, Bonnie did not
come home from school at her usual time.
'Where is she?' Rex asked.
'Don't worry – she probably had
a playdate,' said Woody.

Soon, the door burst open. Bonnie ran
to her table and placed something on top of it.
'What is that strange metal contraption?'
Buzz whispered to Woody.
They watched as Bonnie undid a small latch...

...and spun around with a small, furry creature in her hands.

Bonnie had brought home the Sunnyside Daycare classroom pet – a hamster named Harvey!

Bonnie cuddled the little animal, then ran out of the room with it.

'She'll never play with us now!' wailed Rex. 'We're not cute and cuddly.'

'Speak for yourself,' replied Trixie.

'Calm down, everyone!' Buzz reassured them. 'Bonnie's got a new pet, but we're still her toys.'

That night, Bonnie didn't play
with her toys. She only played
with Harvey, the hamster.
She dressed him up...

and took him to a tea party.

She even kissed him goodnight.

When Bonnie left for school the next day,
the toys decided they had to do something if
they wanted her to play with them that night.

'I'll have a talk with the fuzzy little guy,'
said Woody. He began to fiddle with the latch
on Harvey's cage.

'Umm, Woody, maybe you should keep
that shut,' warned Buzz.

But Woody opened the door – and
the hamster zipped out of the cage,
onto the floor and out of Bonnie's room!

'Woody! How could you let him out?'
cried Jessie.

'I didn't do it on purpose!' said Woody.

'Bonnie loves that hamster,' said Buzz.
'We've got to find him before she gets home
from school.'

Together, the toys tiptoed down the
hall. Suddenly, a furry head poked
out of a nearby doorway.

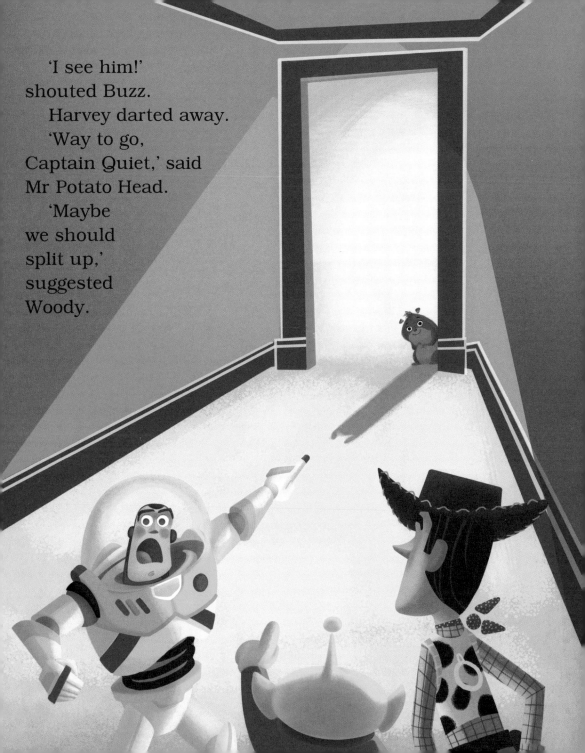

'I see him!'
shouted Buzz.
    Harvey darted away.
    'Way to go,
Captain Quiet,' said
Mr Potato Head.
    'Maybe
we should
split up,'
suggested
Woody.

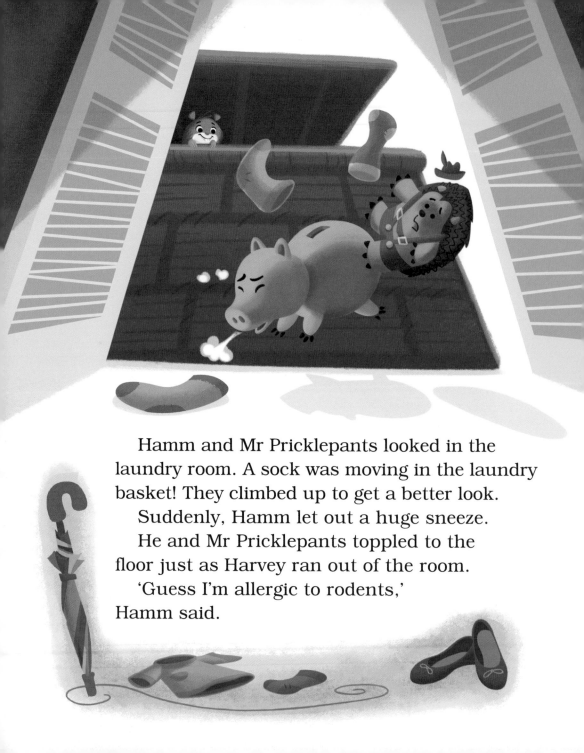

Hamm and Mr Pricklepants looked in the laundry room. A sock was moving in the laundry basket! They climbed up to get a better look.

Suddenly, Hamm let out a huge sneeze.

He and Mr Pricklepants toppled to the floor just as Harvey ran out of the room.

'Guess I'm allergic to rodents,' Hamm said.

Trixie and Mr Potato Head were looking under the beds when Trixie spotted two eyes peering at her.

She wiggled farther under the bed. And then... 'Uh-oh – I'm stuck!'

Mr Potato Head started tugging on Trixie's legs, until POP! He lost his arms!

The pair didn't even notice when Harvey darted away.

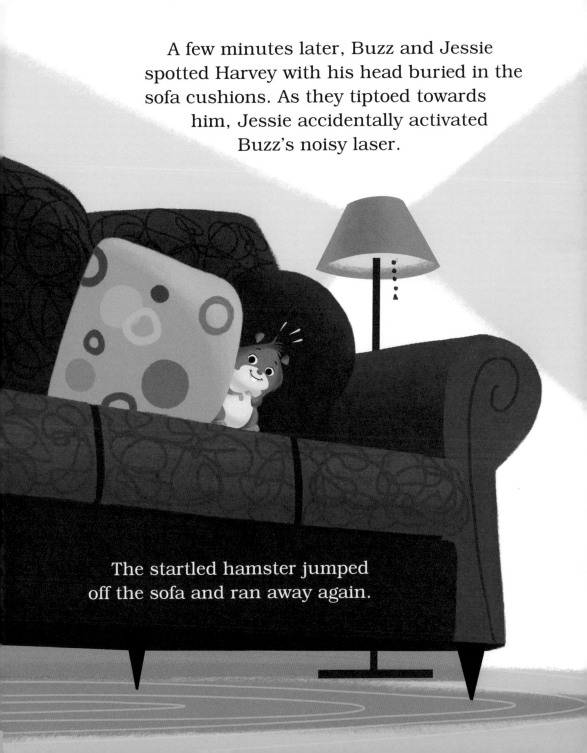

A few minutes later, Buzz and Jessie spotted Harvey with his head buried in the sofa cushions. As they tiptoed towards him, Jessie accidentally activated Buzz's noisy laser.

The startled hamster jumped off the sofa and ran away again.

All the toys met in the kitchen. They
asked Chuckles if he had seen the hamster.
   'Is he small, furry, kind of round?'
asked Chuckles.
   'That's him!' said Mrs Potato Head.
   'Nope – haven't seen him,' said Chuckles.
   Just then, the toys heard a noise coming
from a cupboard. Woody opened the wooden
door and found Harvey happily munching
on some breakfast cereal.

'Okay, Harvey!' said Woody. 'Time
to go back to Bonnie's room.'
    But the hamster just kept nibbling
on his cereal.

            'Come on, little critter!'
            Jessie swung her lasso
            around the hamster and
            tugged gently. But Harvey
            wouldn't budge.

Suddenly, Buzz had an idea. 'Everyone grab a few pieces of cereal, then follow me,' he said.

Buzz began placing pieces of cereal in a line across the kitchen floor. He was making a trail! The other toys followed.

When the hamster saw the cereal on the kitchen floor, he climbed out of the cupboard and nibbled his way through the kitchen...

down the hallway...

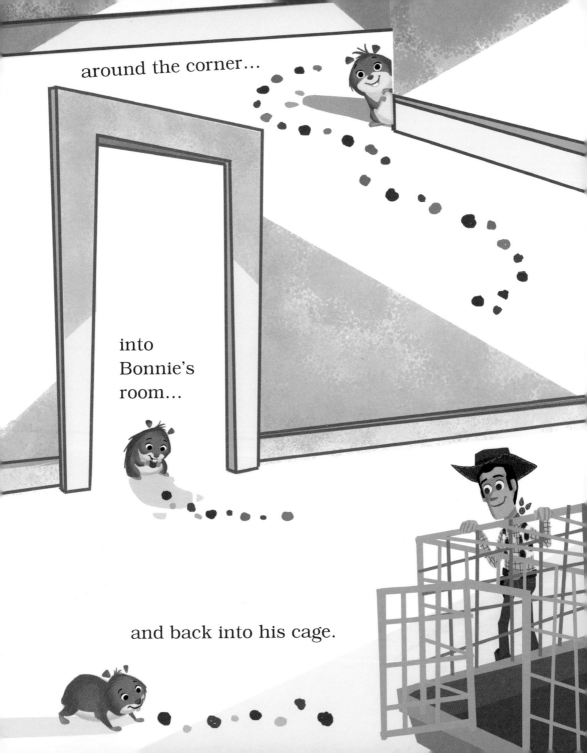

around the corner...

into
Bonnie's
room...

and back into his cage.

The toys cheered. They were glad to have Harvey back where he belonged – even if that meant Bonnie wouldn't have time to play with them.

Suddenly, the toys heard a car door slam.
'Bonnie's home!' they cried. Everyone took
their places as Bonnie burst into her room and
ran to the hamster cage.

'Hello, Harvey! Are you ready to meet your
new friends?' she asked.

The toys were surprised when Bonnie
introduced them to the hamster one by one.

'We're all going to play together every day!'
she said.

Soon, the toys loved Harvey just as much as Bonnie did.

'I think playtime is more fun with Harvey here,' said Woody.

'You're right,' Buzz replied. 'But let's keep extra cereal around just in case.'

Treasure Cove Stories

Book list may be subject to change.